FairYouth
Emylee of Forest Springs

A Novel by
Christine Dzidrums

Additional Writing by
Leah Rendon

CREATIVE MEDIA, INC.
PO Box 6270
Whittier, California 90609-6270
United States of America

www.CREATIVEMEDIA.NET

Cover and Book design by Joseph Dzidrums
Illustrations by Lyle Lopez

First Printing: April 2012

Library of Congress Control Number: 2012905353

ISBN 978-1-938438-05-9   10 9 8 7 6 5 4 3 2 1

FairYouth
Emylee of Forest Springs

A Novel by
Christine Dzidrums

Additional Writing by
Leah Rendon

Dedicated to my children

Chapter 1
Jessamine

When the Fay sisters arrived in sleepy little Forest Springs, I never dreamed they were fairies. And if anyone had claimed they were, I'd have rolled my eyes in disbelief. And then I'd have rolled them a second time for good measure. After all, how many 12-year-olds still believe in fairies?

Fairies exist in children's stories, not the real world. They fly using delicate wings, clutch glittery wands and sprinkle pixie dust everywhere. Such mythical creatures flutter about the universe granting wishes and casting magic spells.

Fairies don't look like Jessamine or Leiko or Reva, my gorgeous classmates at Forest Springs Middle School. They don't sit beside me in Pre-Algebra struggling to solve frustrating equations, like us mortals.

That's why their staggering revelation floored me. The Fay sisters came to Forest Springs for one reason - me. Me - the girl who never existed. Me - the invisible loner.

But it's true. The Fays purposefully sought my friendship. I was their mission.

When Jessamine sauntered into my biology class on her first day at Forest Springs Middle School, several boys almost tumbled out of their chairs ogling her. The leggy teenager boasted luxurious red locks, milky skin and stunning blue eyes. In short, she defined beautiful.

Though only thirteen years old, Jessamine oozed elegance and sophistication. Wearing a flowing gold dress with black tights and matching Victorian boots, she resembled a supermodel.

"I'm sorry," I imagined our biology teacher, Mr. Ryley, saying. "This class is for gawky middle school students. You belong on a fashion runway instead."

"Class, we have a new student," he announced. "Please welcome Jessamine Fay."

The class murmured their welcomes. Several girls self-consciously smoothed their hair. Some guys uttered hello a little louder than necessary.

If Jessamine noticed her dazzling affect, she didn't show it. Instead she smiled radiantly and offered a friendly wave.

"We're reviewing chapter seven in preparation for tomorrow's lab experiment," Mr. Ryley said, handing her a worn textbook.

"Take a seat," he continued pleasantly. "You may choose any table with an empty chair."

Upon hearing those words, head cheerleader Melanie Kristopher sat up straighter and patted the empty seat next to her. I knew when her BFF, Tessa Chow, returned from her bout with the stomach flu, she would need a new lab partner. After all, Melanie would betray even her closest friends and family just to preserve her status as Forest Springs' most popular middle school student.

Except Jessamine bypassed Melanie and stood by my table instead.

"May I sit here?" she smiled.

Some classmates actually gasped. Others, like Melanie, watched with wide eyes.

"Of course," I squeaked.

People rarely spoke to me, much less singled me out. When I glanced around the classroom, 22 shocked adolescents were wondering why the new girl had approached me.

Jessamine slipped gracefully into the chair next to mine and flashed me a dazzling smile. I responded by burying my face in my studies.

"I'm Jessamine," she whispered, although I already knew her name.

I should have introduced myself in return. Except being socially awkward, I just nodded, twirled my long blonde pony-tail around my index finger and stared at my book.

After an insufferably long pause, the persistent Jessamine attempted yet again to make chit chat.

"What's your name?" she asked.

"Emylee," I answered.

"That's a pretty name," Jessamine said. "I like it. It's very traditional. Classic."

"Thanks," I muttered.

"Nowadays, people have the strangest names," she continued. "I once met a girl named Tangerine. Isn't that odd?"

The only thing odd was this gorgeous girl wasting her time on a wallflower like me. It didn't make sense. I just smiled and nodded.

"Of course, she was from Florida," Jessamine laughed. "Maybe that's why her parents named her after a citrus fruit."

I forced a laugh. It sounded stiff and unnatural. I fidgeted and glanced at the wall clock. Thankfully class had ended, and I could make my escape.

"But who am I to judge?" she continued. "My name is unusual, too."

"Class, bring your lab equipment tomorrow," Mr. Ryley announced, as rowdy students slammed books and folders into their backpacks.

"It's lunchtime, right?" Jessamine asked. "I better find my sisters."

"You have sisters?" I asked in surprise.

"Two," she smiled.

I nodded and threw my messenger bag over my shoulder.

"Well it was nice to..."

Before I could finish, Jessamine stood and linked her arm in mine.

"Let's go find them," she smiled.

Chapter 2
Leiko and Reva

"We lived in Winter Park, Florida, before we moved here," Jessamine said, while we waited in the lunch line.

Though I'd brown bagged my lunch, like always, I waited with Jessamine in the cafeteria.

"Cheese pizza and a fruit cup, please," she cheerfully told the counter worker, who gave her a double take before nodding.

The line seemed eerily silent. Heads tilted in our new classmate's direction, eavesdropping on each word that spilled from her lips.

"It's an Orlando suburb," she continued. "I loved it. It's very cultural. They host an amazing sidewalk art festival every year that attracts thousands."

I nodded trying to look impressed but instead felt very distracted. Why had this new girl, out of my league on the social ladder, taken an interest in me?

"They also host a yearly Bach Festival," she added. "Do you like Bach?"

"What song does he sing?" I asked.

Jessamine wrinkled her brow. Then she giggled softly in a friendly manner.

"Johann Sebastian Bach," she smiled. "The German composer."

I felt like the world's biggest idiot. Bach. Classical musical. Of course I knew who he was.

"Right, Bach," I said. "Sure, I know him."

"Well, I don't know him," I clarified. "I know his music."

Jessamine handed cash to a student cashier who eyed her approvingly. No doubt her undeniable beauty struck him.

"Cool bracelet," he admired, motioning to a gothic silver band that she wore.

"Thank you, Sir," Jessamine replied appreciatively as she lifted her food tray from the counter. "It's Victorian. It's a family heirloom."

We then walked outside into our school's courtyard.

"Where do you usually sit?" Jessamine asked.

"I always eat lunch in the library," I answered.

"Oh, but it's such a beautiful day," Jessamine replied enthusiastically. "It's too lovely outside to be stuck inside a dull building."

"Jessamine, over here," a sharp voice called.

I scanned the lunch area. My eyes landed on a Japanese girl with short, choppy blue hair and matching lipstick. She wore a plaid miniskirt, baggy t-shirt, dark tights and black combat boots. She waved impatiently.

"That's my sister," Jessamine informed me. "Let's sit with her."

I felt unnerved, scared. Jessamine's sister looked intimidating. She appraised me carefully as we walked toward her.

"Greetings, Leiko," Jessamine chirped, sliding gracefully onto a bench. "Let me introduce you to Emylee. She's my biology partner."

"Hey," Leiko replied casually.

"Hi," I answered meekly.

"How's your first day going?" Jessamine asked, as she bit eagerly into her pizza.

"Painfully," Leiko answered, sucking a lemon. "I'm taking creative writing. Kill me now."

"That sounds fun," Jessamine replied wistfully. "I would love that class."

"I wanted ceramics," Leiko said. "But that class was full, so now I'm stuck with loners who write depressing poems."

After making the last comment, Leiko grew quiet and glanced guiltily at me.

Interesting. I wasn't surprised that Leiko guessed my friendless status. But why had she worried about hurting my feelings?

13

"I write poetry," Jessamine smiled. "It's a perfect outlet for one's emotions."

"The only thing I hate more than creative writing is P.E.," Leiko said. "And I have it next period. Yuck."

"But you're good at sports," Jessamine remarked. "Not like me. I'm dreading P.E."

I nibbled my cheese sandwich, hoping that neither sister would ask me a question next. I hated small talk.

"Most people are horrible athletes," Leiko snorted. "That's why I hate P.E. I'll be playing organized sports with klutzes."

"I'll bet you're good at sports," Jessamine smiled, turning toward me. "You have an athletic body."

I shook my head and sipped my apple juice. I hoped my stall tactic would encourage them to continue their conversation without me, but they waited for me to expand on my non-verbal response.

"No," I answered. "I hate sports."

"Hello," a voice greeted.

A dark-haired Hispanic girl set her lunch bag on the table. She wore a cute purple mini dress. Her dark, wavy hair was pinned back with a studded barrette. Though the girl lacked Jessamine's elegant looks, she was still quite pretty. She smiled warmly at me, and I immediately felt at ease.

"Emylee, meet my other sister, Reva," Jessamine said.

"I'm pleased to make your acquaintance," she replied.

"Hi," I answered.

Jessamine and Reva possessed a formal quality that made them appear older than their years.

"Jessamine, are you eating pizza?" Reva asked disapprovingly.

Jessamine giggled softly and threw her hands up defensively.

"Guilty as charged," she remarked.

Reva frowned and shook her head in disgust. She opened a recyclable lunch bag and fished out a plastic container containing a garden salad.

"This pizza is so cheesy," Jessamine raved, taking another bite. "And sooo good."

"And sooo bad for you," Reva frowned.

"Who cares," Leiko chimed in. "It's Jessamine's body. If she wants to eat french fries ten times a day, that's her business. It's no skin off your back."

"For the record, I would never eat fatty foods ten times a day," Jessamine laughed. "That's disgusting."

"Well if you did, that's on you," Leiko commented. "Not Reva."

"But as her sister, I look out for her," Reva pointed out. "I offered to make her a healthy lunch this morning, but she refused."

"And I love your cooking," Jessamine complimented, sucking stringy cheese wrapped around her finger. "But today I wanted something fattening, greasy and delicious."

"Are you taking any cool classes, Reva?" Leiko asked.

"I just came from Advanced Algebra," she answered.

"Advanced Algebra?" Leiko laughed. "I'm barely taking Pre-Algebra."

"I am a year older than you," Reva reminded her.

"But Advanced Algebra," Leiko said. "That's so… advanced."

"Are there many people in your class?" Jessamine asked.

"Only four," Reva admitted.

"Wow," Jessamine said with admiration. "That's Reva, our intellectual giant!"

"More like a freak," Leiko snickered.

"Be nice, Leiko," Jessamine scolded. "We're blessed to have a genius in our family."

"I'm not a genius," Reva protested.

"Yes, you are," Jessamine insisted. "Embrace it."

"Have you lived in Forest Springs all your life, Emylee?" Reva asked, changing the subject.

I finished chewing and nodded. Then I wiped my lips to ensure I didn't have any food on them.

"All my life," I answered.

"So what's it like here?" she prodded. "We just arrived on Saturday."

16

"It's your average New England town," I answered. "It's probably not as bustling as Florida."

"Or as humid," Leiko chimed.

"Do you live with your parents?" Jessamine asked.

"I live with my mom," I answered, praying they wouldn't pry any further.

"Are you all adopted?" I blurted, half-curious, half-hoping to derail the existing topic.

"How did you ever guess?" Leiko answered with mock incredulousness.

"Pay no attention to our cranky sister," Reva said, rolling her eyes. "She's just grumpy because she misses her boyfriend."

"I am not grumpy, and I do not miss my boyfriend," Leiko protested defensively.

"You'll have to excuse Leiko," Jessamine laughed. "She's been in a foul mood for 12 years."

"Ha ha ha," Leiko shot back sarcastically. "You might want to skip a career in stand up comedy."

"To answer your question, Emylee," Jessamine continued, still giggling. "Yes, we are all adopted, but you'd never know it. We argue just as much as blood-related siblings."

"And we would do anything for each other," Reva added. "Even Miss Crabby Pants over there would stand in front of a bus to save us."

"That depends," Leiko replied. "How big is the bus?"

"Your bearcat exterior doesn't fool us," Reva answered, shaking her head.

"Bearcat?" I asked. "What's a bearcat?"

Reva froze. My question clearly unnerved her.

"Bearcat refers to a girl with a fiery personality," she responded, wearing a strained expression.

"How funny," I said. "I've never heard that word."

"So do you have any brothers or sisters?" Jessamine asked suddenly.

"No," I answered. "I'm an only child."

And alone in the world.

"Do you have extended family?" Reva asked.

"It's just Mom and me," I said.

"So where are you living?" I asked.

With all the swift topic changes, I felt like the Fay sisters and I were playing an intense ping-pong game.

"We live north of uptown," Leiko answered. "It's an isolated area. I love it."

"You should come over," Reva said. "Our mom would love to meet you."

"I'd like that," I lied.

"How about today?" Jessamine asked.

"I work today," I said, grateful for the truth.

"You have a job?" a surprised Reva asked. "That's swell. I didn't think businesses hired people our age."

"My boss and grandmother were good friends," I answered. "She probably took pity on me."

"Was?" Jessamine asked.

"My grandma died several years ago," I answered, a pang shooting through me.

"I'm sorry," Jessamine replied softly. "I can tell you loved her very much."

Overcome with sadness, I shrugged so I wouldn't have to speak.

"Where do you work?" Leiko asked, after an awkward moment.

"At Second Chance," I answered. "It's a thrift store. I help Mrs. Miller, the owner, behind the counter twice a week."

"I love thrift shops," Leiko said, perking up. "I spend hours in them."

"You should see her closet," Reva added. "She owns many second hand clothes."

"Gently-used clothing has character," Leiko replied. "Not like those items found in the stuffy boutiques you and Jessamine like."

"To each their own," Jessamine smiled.

"Where is Second Chance located?" Reva asked.

"On 4th and Destiny in downtown," I answered.

"I'll go with you today," Reva said to the youngest sister.

"Score," Leiko exclaimed, pumping her fist excitedly.

"Are you coming, Jessamine?" Reva asked.

"I can't," she answered. "I have cheerleading tryouts after school. Some girls invited me to audition."

The spirit squad was a tight-knit clique that protected their territory fiercely. That they invited Jessamine to try out spoke volumes about her immediate impact at our school.

I suddenly felt relieved. Jessamine would surely become Forest Springs' newest cheerleader. Soon she would grow tight with the squad members and forget me. Then I could resume my safe, solitary life.

"Why would you waste time with those girls?" Leiko scoffed.

"They seem nice," Jessamine protested. "Besides, I love to dance."

"Then take tango lessons," Leiko said dismissively.

"So I'm wrong to encourage her to eat better, but you can chastise her for cheerleading?" an annoyed Reva asked.

"Geez, Reva," Leiko sputtered. "Mind your own business."

"I could say the same thing," she shot back.

"Maybe you both should calm down," Jessamine suggested nervously.

"No one is talking to you," Leiko told her.

"Excuse me," a hurt Jessamine replied. "This concerns me. I have every right to speak."

The three sisters began squabbling again. Just as I debated slinking away unnoticed, Reva raised her hand authoritatively.

"Girls," she urged. "Let's not argue in front of our new friend."

Jessamine smoothed her hair and smiled, while Leiko pursed her lips tightly.

Friend? Me? I barely knew them.

Panic washed over me. I had spent years as a content loner. Yet in mere hours, three unique, colorful sisters had stormed into my life, and it didn't seem like they were leaving any time soon.

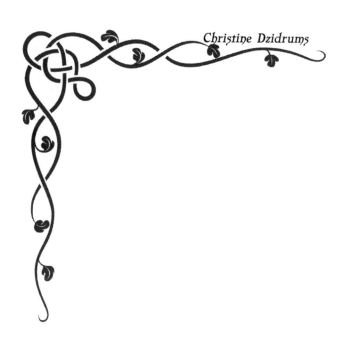

Christine Dzidrums

Stranger

How can we help?
Lost in this world
What will we find
When your mystery is unfurled?

Can we save you from the future?
Help you close the past?
Find the perfect ending
With promises so vast.

Hold on tight
The pain will cease
Trust us with your fears
You will find peace.

Written by Jessamine Fay

Christine Dzidrums

Chapter 3
Second Chance

The two Fay sisters spent nearly an hour at Second Chance. Leiko scrutinized every garment on each rack, while Reva followed her patiently.

After trying on about 30 outfits, Leiko approached the cash register carrying a mountain of clothes. Among her purchases: a vintage black leather jacket, six miniskirts and nine blouses, including a striped silk shirt with worn buttons.

"Yuck," Reva remarked, eyeing the offensive blouse. "That's hideous."

"It's attrocious," Leiko agreed. "But this was the last owner's lucky shirt, so I'm snatching it up."

"How would you know that?" a bewildered Mrs. Miller asked, punching cash register buttons.

"Uh, it's just a hunch," Leiko answered quickly.

Reva shot her sister a dirty look.

"What an awesome store," Leiko raved, eyeing the thrift shop approvingly.

"Thank you," Mrs. Miller smiled. "We just celebrated our 40th anniversary."

Leiko looked very pretty when she wasn't pouting or frowning. The Fay sisters had clearly won the gene jackpot.

My shift ended just as Mrs. Miller handed Leiko her new purchases.

"We'll walk you home," Reva said. "We're dying to see more of this town. Right, Leiko?"

"Um...sure," she replied unconvincingly.

"That's not necessary," I answered. "I live in the opposite direction of your house."

"We insist," Reva answered firmly.

Ten minutes later, we headed toward my house. Leiko chatted happily about her new outfits, while Reva seemed distracted. As the city sidewalk faded into a dirt road, we neared Forest Springs' infamous blind hill, a source of many traffic accidents throughout the years. Sure enough, a car of rowdy high school students came barreling over the slope at lightning speed. The car soared through the air before slamming back onto the road, veering dangerously close to us. The passengers laughed excitedly as they sped away.

"Watch where you're going," Leiko shouted.

"That was exciting," Reva remarked dryly.

As we reached the hilltop, I prayed the girls wouldn't invite themselves inside my house. I also hoped my mother was at work today.

"Will your mom be home?" Reva asked, as if reading my thoughts.

"She's probably sleeping," I lied. "She isn't feeling well today."

"I'm sorry to hear that," she replied. "Does your mother get sick often?"

"Not really," I replied.

"What about your father?" Reva asked. "Where does he live?"

Sometimes Reva and Jessamine's questions felt like the third degree.

"He's a salesman so he travels all the time," I fibbed. "He doesn't visit often, but he calls all the time."

I couldn't tell the truth. That my mom didn't love me and I'd never met my dad.

My grandmother raised me for the first seven years of my life. She adored me, and I loved her dearly. While Grandma cared for me, Mom partied every night and slept through each day.

Shortly after I turned seven, doctors diagnosed my grand-mother with advanced lung cancer. When she received her fatal prognosis, Grandma stressed over my future and ordered Mom to get her act together. My mother vowed to change but I never believed her. She had already disappointed me too many times.

I spent Grandma's final year of life reassuring her that everything would be fine. As her disease progressed, she became weaker and weaker. One evening, I held her hand while she slipped away forever.

Mom shed many tears when Grandma died. I wondered if she grieved the loss of her mother or her loss of independence. Mom assumed a parental role at first. For several months she actually stopped drinking and held a steady job. After a while, though, alcohol beckoned again, and she resumed her destructive habits.

I kept Mom's non-existent parental supervision a secret so social services wouldn't get involved. Being bounced around various foster homes sounded horrifying. So instead I pretended everything was fine. I always hoped to one day earn a college scholarship and leave Forest Springs forever.

When the Fay sisters and I finally reached my home, I forced a carefree smile. Inside, though, I vowed to keep them out of my house.

"I'm glad you liked Second Chance, Leiko," I said. "I'll tell you when any new items arrive."

"That would be epic," she answered.

I turned to Reva who studied my home's dead lawn and shabby exterior.

"I'd invite you inside but Mom has a horrible migraine," I lied.

"I'm sorry to hear that," Reva replied. "Our mom gets migraines, too. They're horribly debilitating."

"You can say that again," I answered. "There are days when Mom can't get off the couch and go to work."

"Green tea and hot compresses help," she suggested.

"That's a good idea," I answered, hoping they would just leave.

"I can come inside and make her tea," Reva offered.

"That's okay," I said swiftly. "I've got it covered. Thanks."

"It's no problem at all," she insisted. "We want to help."

I snuck a look at Leiko. She looked bored and eager to leave.

"Thank you, but Mom's uncomfortable having company when she isn't feeling well," I answered.

"Well...okay," a reluctant Reva replied.

"Thanks for your suggestions, though," I told her.

"Since our mother has experience coping with migraines," Reva continued. "Maybe she can stop by sometime and talk to your mother?"

"Well, Mom sees a doctor for her migraines," I answered. "But if she ever needs a second opinion, I'll tell her about your mother."

Reva lingered by my front porch hesitantly, while Leiko grew more and more restless.

"Well," Reva finally said. "See you at school tomorrow. I hope your mom feels better really soon."

"Thanks again," I answered.

I waited until Reva and Leiko settled back on the dirt road before I entered my house. As Mom slept on the couch, the television blared a payday loans commercial. I grabbed the remote and turned off the power. The electric bills wouldn't pay themselves.

I walked to the kitchen and grabbed an apple from the fridge. My mind wandered to the Fay sisters. Their mother had not only wanted them, she chose

them. Plus, they were beautiful, popular and spent their afternoons shopping. They certainly led charmed lives.

A strange feeling haunted me. Questions nagged and taunted. Why had Jessamine befriended me? Reva seemed anxious to meet Mom. Why? What could three perfect sisters want from boring me?

Chapter 4
Negative

"Boy were you obvious," Leiko snorted.

"Pardon me?" Reva asked, as they walked back toward town.

"You practically stormed into her house," Leiko scoffed.

"I did not," Reva reacted defensively. "Besides, you weren't any help. You spent all day focusing on yourself and not Emylee."

"Someone had to act normal," Leiko shrugged. "You and Jessamine smothered the poor girl."

"Should we drag our feet?" Reva demanded. "What if a catastrophe happens before we can intervene?"

"Next time be more subtle," Leiko grumbled.

"The blue-haired girl preaches about subtlety," Reva laughed. "How fitting."

Leiko stopped suddenly and glared at her sister.

"Stop bashing my dye job," she snapped. "My hair color isn't hurting anyone."

"It draws looks," Reva argued. "We should blend in with our classmates, not scream for attention."

"Excuse me for having style," Leiko hissed. "I know that's a foreign concept to you."

"I have style," Reva answered.

"Whatever helps you sleep at night."

"Oh, I don't have style?"

"You're very…old-fashioned."

"I prefer to think of my look as classic," a hurt Reva responded.

"Classically boring," Leiko laughed.

"You can be so cruel sometimes."

"You started it."

"Why don't you just stop talking?" Reva lashed out, as she began walking again.

"My pleasure," Leiko shot back.

The two sisters resumed walking side-by-side in steamed silence.

When Reva and Leiko entered Burger Works, they spotted their beautiful sister in a corner booth. A good-looking teenager wearing a varsity jacket sat flirting with her.

"No, honestly," Jessamine insisted. "We just moved to Forest Springs. I don't have a phone number yet."

"Beat it, Kid," Leiko ordered.

"His name is Colin," an embarrassed Jessamine told her.

The jock examined Leiko carefully.

"Cool hair," he praised.

"Yeah, yeah," Leiko replied impatiently. "Beat it, Colin."

"Leiko, mind your manners," Jessamine blushed.

"I'm too hungry to be polite," Leiko stated.

"What's your problem?" Colin asked defensively.

"You're my problem," Leiko told him. "You're sitting in my seat."

Colin stood up, shaking his head in disgust.

"Fine," he replied, before turning to Jessamine. "See you later, Beautiful"

Leiko gagged as she and Reva slid into the red booth.

"That was a high school boy," a crestfallen Jessamine said.

Leiko suddenly shuddered deeply.

"We need to change tables," she announced.

"Why?" Jessamine asked. "This table is fine."

"I'm not sitting here," Leiko insisted.

"How come?" Reva asked.

Leiko scanned the restaurant carefully. Then she leaned close toward her sisters.

"Two people have died in this booth," she whispered.

"Is the food here that bad?" Reva cracked, as Jessamine giggled.

"I'm serious," Leiko replied. "New table. Stat."

"Fine, fine," Jessamine grumbled, standing up.

Seconds later the sisters settled at a different table.

"Thanks for chasing away a high school boy," Jessamine said, barely missing a beat.

"You're too young for that cad," Reva responded dismissively.

"Or too old," Leiko laughed.

"I liked him," Jessamine said. "And you scared him away."

"You think you liked him," Reva replied. "But after your first date, you would find a million annoying things about him and lose complete interest."

"She's right," Leiko agreed. "The relationship wouldn't last longer than a day."

"You don't know that," Jessamine argued. "He could be 'the one.'"

"How would you know 'the one' anyway?" Leiko asked. "You've never been in love."

"She's never let herself fall in love," Reva clarified.

Jessamine looked down in embarrassment and sipped water. She used a spoon to inspect her reflection and then turned to her sisters.

"I went to Yeoman's Grocery Store after tryouts," she announced. "I bought a candy bar from Emylee's mother and took a reading."

"Well?" Reva asked.

"She doesn't love Emylee," Jessamine revealed sadly.

"Well we knew that," Reva sighed somberly. "Still, it's good to have confirmation."

"Did you get into her house?" Jessamine asked.

"Negative," Reva answered. "That girl has a stubborn streak."

"Oh dear," Jessamine replied. "This will take more time and effort than we anticipated."

"I'm afraid so," Reva agreed, picking up a menu.

"Great," Leiko groaned. "Now we have to spend more time in this stupid town."

"It's a great town," Jessamine protested. "It's charming and full of history."

"Boring history," Leiko snorted.

"Do you know Forest Springs is a colonial town?" Jessamine asked. "It's over 250 years old."

"Do you know I don't care?" Leiko replied haughtily.

"Leiko, your attitude lately has been horrible, even for you" Jessamine frowned.

"I agree," Reva chimed in. "You're not giving much effort."

"Maybe I don't feel like it," Leiko complained. "I'm sick of traveling everywhere. I hate always being the new girl. I'm tired of helping others."

"You don't have a choice," Reva told her.

"You're right," Leiko said, her voice quivering with anger and sadness. "I didn't choose this life. Reva chose it for me."

"Excuse me for saving your life," Reva snapped.

"Leiko," Jessamine replied softly. "None of us chose this life, but it was our destiny."

"Yeah, yeah," Leiko grumbled. "Sometimes I think Julissa had the right idea."

Reva and Jessamine grew silent at the mention of their former sister. Neither girl spoke for a long time.

"Girls," a tense Reva said. "Let's return to the real issue."

"You're right," Jessamine agreed. "What do you girls think? Can we help Emylee?"

"We don't have a choice," a determined Reva replied. "We must."

"And if we don't succeed?" Leiko asked.

"Then I foresee a huge tragedy," she answered gravely.

Unmoved

My heart feels like a silent bird
That never learned to sing.
My heart snaps like a fallen branch
That dies before each spring.

Though boys have offered love
With gestures or a sign
My heart remains unmoved,
It's never learned to pine

Find me, o' one
Alone I do ache
Show me true love
I am anxious to wake

Written by Jessamine Fay

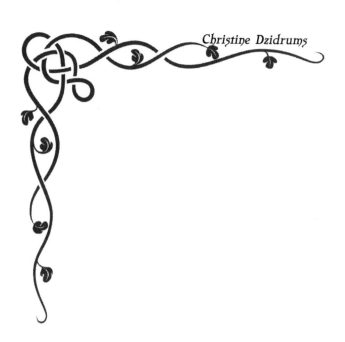

Christine Dzidrums

Chapter 5
Kevin Briggs

Reva, Jessamine and I sat under a white pine tree eating our lunches.

"How did your tryout go?" Reva asked Jessamine, as she munched on a salad.

"I made it," Jessamine announced happily. "They let me know this morning."

"That's great," Reva smiled. "Congratulations."

"I think it'll be fun," Jessamine grinned.

I had hoped that the newest spirit leader might be dining at the popular table now, but no such luck.

When Melanie and her minions approached Jessamine moments earlier and invited her to join them, she politely declined.

"Thank you for the invitation," she answered. "But I'll eat lunch with my sisters and Emylee."

"No problem," Melanie replied, clearly stunned by Jessamine's decision. Before the head cheerleader walked away, she cast a bewildered look at me. Clearly, she, too, could not comprehend Jessamine's loyalty to me.

"Well that was rude," Reva said. "Did she expect you to dump us when she snapped her fingers?"

"Perhaps," Jessamine admitted.

"How can you stomach her?" Reva asked.

"Protect yourself from other people's bad manners by a conspicuous display of your own good ones," Jessamine said calmly.

Like Reva, she sometimes spoke in such old-fashioned ways.

"So where's Leiko?" I asked.

"Who knows," Reva answered. "She's probably making someone's life miserable."

"So what made you move here?" I asked.

Last night, I cooked up a brilliant strategy. I would bombard the Fays with questions so they couldn't poke into my life.

"Our mother just experienced a bad breakup," Reva answered, popping a cucumber slice into her mouth. "She craved a scenery change, so here we are."

"Why Forest Springs?" I asked.

"Our great-grandmother once lived here," Jessamine explained, peeling an orange. "My mom visited here one summer many years ago. She always regarded the town fondly, so here we are."

"And what about your father?" I asked.

"Our parents ended their relationship years ago," Reva answered. "He lives in Upstate New York. We spend every summer with him."

Just then Leiko arrived wearing a black Siouxsie and The Banshees t-shirt and the leather jacket and purple miniskirt from Second Chance.

"Guess what?" she announced triumphantly, plopping down on the grass. "I weaseled out of P.E."

"How did you manage that?" Reva asked.

Leiko pulled a lemon from her pocket, punctured a hole in it and began sucking.

"I joined the track team," she announced.

"The track team," Jessamine said, wrinkling her brow. "But you don't run."

"Oh really, Miss Smarty Pants?" Leiko asked. "I've never run? Not ever? Not once?"

"That's not what I meant," Jessamine clarified, shaking her head. "I meant you've never ran track."

"Well there's a first time for everything, isn't there?"

"Don't be so defensive," Reva said. "We're just surprised by your sudden interest in track."

"I don't have a sudden interest in track," Leiko corrected. "I have a sudden disinterest in P.E."

Reva shrugged, while Jessamine giggled softly.

"So a guy in my English class asked me to the movies," Reva divulged.

Jessamine and Leiko looked up immediately.

"You got asked out before Jessamine did?" a surprised Leiko asked.

"Thanks," Reva glared. "I may not have Jessamine's gorgeous looks, but I'm decent looking."

"That's not what I meant," Leiko explained. "I'm just surprised."

"I'm not Quasimodo."

"You're beautiful," Jessamine assured her. "Everyone knows that."

"I'm glad someone thinks so."

"Oh chill," Leiko told her. "Now you're the one overreacting."

"What's his name?" Jessamine asked.

"Kevin Something," Reva answered, closing one eye while trying to recall his last name.

"Kevin Briggs?" I asked.

"Kevin Briggs," Reva exclaimed. "That's his name. Do you know him?"

Did I know him? I'd only liked Kevin Briggs since kindergarten when he rode a blue trike around the playground.

Six years later, Kevin hadn't changed much. He still sported the same messy, just-stumbled-out-of-bed blond hair. Most people would look sloppy if they adopted the hairstyle but Kevin looked adorable. My heart raced just thinking about his deep blue eyes and lopsided grin.

In the six years that I'd known Kevin, he had spoken to me exactly three times:

"Hey, Emma, can I borrow a number two pencil?"

"Thanks."

"Can I keep this? I have a math test next period."

Okay, so my name isn't Emma but who cares. Kevin Briggs almost knew my name. I could die happy.

"Emylee?" Reva called.

The Fay sisters stared at me. Reva waited patiently, Leiko looked annoyed and Jessamine smiled faintly.

"Do you know Kevin?" Reva repeated.

"Not very well," I admitted. "We were in kindergarten together and shared a music appreciation class last year."

Kevin anchored the popular clique but always behaved differently than his friends. At an age when kids enjoy acting cruel, Kevin rose above such poor behavior. He wasn't some stuck up jerk.

Just last month, Nick Diller, a painfully thin kid with cystic acne, had left the cafeteria with his lunch when our school's star football player, Russ Boor, grabbed his plate of spaghetti from his hands.

"Say 'I'm a zit face' and you'll get it back," the notorious bully commanded, laughing loudly.

Nick turned burgundy. His face froze with shame. He pretended to find the incident funny.

"Ha ha," he laughed unconvincingly. "Very funny, Russ. Now give me back my food."

"Does it look like I'm joking?" Russ asked menacingly. "Now do as I say."

Nick weighed his options. If he called himself a zit face, he would never live it down. On the other hand, if he didn't obey Russ, bye-bye, lunch.

Suddenly, Kevin rose from a nearby bench. He placed a protective hand on Nick's shoulder.

"Hey, Russ," Kevin remarked. "He's a good guy. Give him back his lunch."

"I'm just messing with him," Russ countered. "A little harmless teasing never hurt anyone."

"Nah," Kevin replied. "It's not cool. Cut it out."

The lunch area suddenly became very quiet. Everyone watched intently. Finally, Russ handed back Nick's plate.

"Fine, fine," he said. "Zit Face can have his spaghetti back."

As Nick grabbed his lunch and bolted out of the courtyard, Russ sat back down and attacked a chicken drumstick. Meanwhile Kevin resumed chatting with his buddies as if nothing had happened.

Kevin was cool like that. When he spoke, people listened.
Everyone respected him, even jerks like Russ.

That incident only intensified my feelings for Kevin. He wasn't just good-looking. He also possessed sweet, caring and protective traits.

It bothered me that Kevin liked Reva. It shouldn't have. That perfect specimen didn't know that Emma, if you will, even existed. Even if I sprouted wings, he wouldn't notice me.

Besides, I definitely wasn't his type. All his previous girlfriends were stunning brunettes with strong personalities. With my mousy blonde hair and meek ways, I didn't stand a chance.

I looked up to find Jessamine studying me carefully. A strange chill ran through my body. It felt like she had intruded on my thoughts. When I shifted uncomfortably, she looked away quickly.

"So are you going out with him?" Leiko asked.

I held my breath waiting for Reva's response. Not that her decision affected me.

"Yes, spill the beans," Jessamine begged. "What did you tell him? I'm dying to know!"

"I said I would think about it," Reva shrugged.

I exhaled and relaxed. Was Reva crazy? Who wouldn't jump at the chance to date Kevin Briggs?

"How come?" Leiko demanded. "Isn't he cute?"

"I guess," Reva shrugged. "If you like that type."

Who wouldn't like a gorgeous, sensitive and kind guy?

"What type?" Jessamine asked.

"He's good looking," Reva said thoughtfully. "But we aren't compatible. He's clearly a sports nut, and I'm...not. It would never go anywhere."

"Opposites attract," Jessamine pointed out.

"True," Reva admitted. "But I'd rather not waste my time."

Suddenly the blaring sound of thrashing guitars emanated from Leiko's backpack.

"Time for a new ringtone," Jessamine giggled.

"It's the Ramones," Leiko retorted. "And they are amazing. My ringtone is a lot cooler than that boring classical piece you use."

"Different strokes," Jessamine shrugged.

"It's Joel," Leiko remarked, reading her cell phone.

"I thought you broke up?" Jessamine asked.

"We did," Leiko answered. "I wish he'd leave me alone. I'm so over him."

"No, you're not," Jessamine said softly. "You still love him."

Jessamine stated her words like a fact rather than speculation. Rather than deny her sister's declaration, Leiko just blushed.

"Does Joel also kiss like a duck?" Reva asked, her face twitching in amusement.

Leiko shot Reva a 'shut up or I'll kill you' look.

"Why would you say something like that?" Jessamine asked Reva. "What a strange thing to ask."

"Not really," Reva responded teasingly. "After all, a duck once kissed our sister."

"Reva Fay," Leiko scolded. "How dare you blab that secret!"

"What am I missing?" a confused Jessamine asked.

Reva's eyes danced mischievously, while Leiko looked at the sky and whistled innocently.

"When did you kiss a duck?" Jessamine asked.

Though she posed her question seriously, it sounded so strange that the sisters laughed hysterically at its absurdity. When they finally stopped giggling, Reva spilled the beans.

"Last year, Don Stark kissed Leiko during a field trip to Kennedy Space Center."

"He kissed you?" Jessamine asked, covering her mouth in disbelief.

"Reva, you have a big mouth," Leiko laughed, embarrassed.

"Why am I just discovering this now?" Jessamine asked indignantly.

"It was humiliating" Leiko explained. "I only told Reva because I was dying to tell someone."

"They were watching a film in the theater," Reva explained. "Halfway through the movie, Don leaned over and planted a slimy kiss on her."

"What did you do?" Jessamine asked in mock horror.

"I punched him in the arm," Leiko replied.

"I warned him that if he tried it again, he would talk funny permanently."

Jessamine giggled as she placed her hands daintily over her mouth. Leiko fell backwards onto the grass and laughed. Reva cracked up so hard that she snorted, causing the sisters to howl with laughter.

"You were kissed by Donald Duck," Jessamine gasped.

"He kissed you with his beak," Reva exclaimed, wiping away tears.

The Fay sisters disintegrated into laughter again. They laughed so hard that several classmates threw them amused smiles.

I watched Jessamine, Reva and Leiko attentively. Sure they often bickered, but they clearly loved each other and enjoyed one another's company. For the first time in ages, I envied someone — three people, to be exact.

I imagined being a Fay sister. Being so beautiful that people stopped talking when you entered the room. Being so interesting that Kevin Briggs wanted to date you. Being so confident that you dyed your hair shocking blue.

But I reminded myself that I'd never be like the Fay girls. Because for every Jessamine, Reva and Leiko that existed, there were thousands of girls like me: plain, forgettable and forgotten.

Leiko Fay
Creative Writing
Period 4
Friday the 12th

Assignment: Right Now I feel...

trapped in a strange, boring town! Why can't we ever move to New York City, Los Angeles, Seattle or Chicago? Why are we stuck in Nowheresville?

Today I was at my locker, when some punk walked by and snickered, "Nice blue hair, Cookie Monster."

I replied, "I'm impressed. I didn't think you had learned your colors yet."

I wish I'd snapped a picture of his lobster red face as he scuffled off. What a loser.

I haven't found one cool kid at this school yet. I doubt anyone here has heard of The Clash or Siouxsie and the Banshees. Earlier some girl in my history class glanced at my t-shirt and asked me if the Ramones was a TV show. Seriously? I could teach her some true history about great punk bands from the 1970s, but she probably wouldn't appreciate it.

Get me outta here!!!!!!!!!

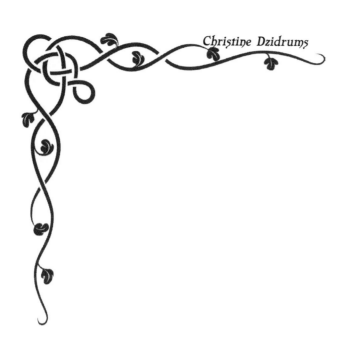

Christine Dzidrums

Chapter 6
Being Strong

Mrs. Miller canceled my shift today. Despite Leiko's earlier shopping binge, sales were dismal this week, so I lost hours.

Bummer. I needed the cash. Because Mom never turns off the television or lights, our electric bill soared this month. Plus she missed work several times this week, seriously hurting our cash flow.

Faced with a free afternoon, I opted to clean. First I deposited Mom's empty beer bottles into our recycle bin. Then I emptied the week's trash into the outside garbage can. Afterwards I packed the dishwasher with dirty plates and cups.

Just as I finished, Mom burst through the back door. Her hair resembled a rat's nest. Smeared mascara accentuated the heavy bags under her eyes. She'd obviously just finished partying hard.

My stomach lurched. Anxiety overcame me. Would Mom be confrontational, or would she simply ignore me?

"Hi Mom," I greeted her, trying to sound cheerful.

"Morning," she muttered, tossing her purse on the floor and heading for the living room.

Seconds later, the television turned on. No doubt Mom was watching some reality TV show and would eventually pass out halfway through the episode.

I sighed and wiped my hands on a dishtowel. At least Mom hadn't behaved belligerently. I'd always rather she ignore me than pick an argument.

I wrung my hands and surveyed our cramped two-bedroom house. When Grandma lived here, it felt like a home. The floors sparkled. Dishes never piled in the sink. Clutter didn't exist. Some days I arrived home to the heavenly scent of oatmeal raisin cookies.

Sometimes when Grandma felt particularly lenient, she let me sample dessert before dinner. She'd pour a glass of cold milk and place two cookies on a white cocktail napkin.

"Good day at school, Emybelle?" she always asked.

"Yup," I answered, licking sugar off each cookie before taking a bite.

"Did you break any hearts?"

"Four or five," I usually replied, which always garnered a laugh.

Tears now clouded my eyes. I took our chats for granted back then. Now I would give anything to hear Grandma's voice one last time. I missed her terribly. I shoved aside overwhelming emotions and shook my head in disgust.

Be strong, Emylee. Crying won't help you one bit.

Grandma always called me her precious china doll. When she died, pieces of me chipped away and left me broken. Now I keep myself safely hidden, so the rest of me won't shatter. So others can't discard me... as Mom did.

Leiko Fay
Creative Writing
Period 4
Monday the 15th

Assignment: I wish...

I wish...I could be normal.

I wish...I could forge lasting friendships.

I wish...I could bleed.

I wish...I could remain in one place longer than a few months.

I wish...I could go to a senior prom.

I wish...I could go to college and live in a dorm and gain the freshman 15.

I wish...I could get married.

I wish...I could have children someday.

I would...I could march in a high school graduation ceremony.

I wish...I were real.

Chapter 7
Speed

Jessamine, Reva and I watched Leiko prepare for her first track meet. Ever the individualist, the stubborn 12-year-old wore a black bandana on her right arm in an attempt to dress up (or perhaps protest?) the school's blue and gold uniforms.

As Jessamine massaged her calves, several male track team members spent more time watching her than warming up. If the beautiful Fay sister noticed the attention, she never uttered a word. Meanwhile, Reva read a copy of *The Great Gatsby*.

"Cheerleading is exhausting," Jessamine grumbled. "Our cheer advisor acts like a drill sergeant."

"Mmm hmm," Reva answered, absorbed in her book.

"She made us run stairs for 20 minutes because we messed up our pyramid," Jessamine continued.

"Beauty is a burden," Reva answered, her nose buried in F. Scott Fitzgerald's masterpiece.

"What's that supposed to mean?"

Jessamine asked. "Cheerleading isn't about looking pretty. It's physically demanding. You should try it."

"I've no interest in wearing tiny skirts and waving pom-poms at dumb jocks," Reva responded.

"Because that's all cheerleaders do," Jessamine shot back sarcastically. "We don't perform amazing lifts and difficult acrobatics."

Meanwhile, a few feet away, Kevin Briggs stretched in anticipation of his run. His shaggy blond hair nearly covered his mischievous eyes. He looked tanner than usual, probably from spending so much time outside playing sports.

Suddenly Kevin looked directly at me and smiled. I looked away quickly, but it was too late. My crush had caught me ogling him. I felt mortified.

"Right, Emylee?" a voice asked.

I looked up startled. Jessamine waited for me expectantly.

"What was the question?" I asked.

"Cheerleading takes talent, right?" Jessamine repeated patiently. "It's not just about looking pretty and waving pompoms."

"Right," I answered. "I can't do those hard flips and scary pyramids."

"Thank you," Jessamine said.

"I'm totally teasing," Reva said, stretching. "Cheerleading requires a clear understanding of physics. You have to master weight balance, angular momentum and so on."

"I don't really think you're all Dumb Doras," she added.

"Dumb who?" I asked.

"Dumb Dora," she admitted reluctantly.

"Who is Dora?" I asked, my curiosity piqued.

"Dumb Dora is an expression for a stupid female," Reva replied, looking strained.

"I've never heard it," I answered. "Dumb Dora. That's funny. I'll have to borrow it."

"I must have heard that phrase from my grandmother," she responded abruptly.

"So how's work, Emylee?" Jessamine asked.

Somehow I suspected the girls were purposefully changing the subject, but I didn't know why. Meanwhile the first track event began.

"Slowly," I answered. "Business stinks. I'm barely logging any hours."

"How's your mom's migraine?" Reva asked.

"She's much better," I lied.

Now I would change the subject.

"Did you ever give Kevin Briggs an answer?" I asked Reva.

"Yes," Jessamine perked up. "Are you going out with him?"

Reva groaned and scoped the area to ensure that Kevin wasn't within earshot. He now stood several feet away laughing with a teammate.

"I haven't answered yet," she whispered.

"He's a nice guy, but I don't consider him…you know… the cat's meow."

The cat's meow? Reva certainly used interesting expressions.

"I get it," Jessamine joked. "He's tall, good looking, athletic and an all-around nice guy. I can understand why you wouldn't date him."

I agreed with Jessamine but didn't say anything. I had kept my crush a secret for years and intended to keep it that way.

"He brought me a rose from his mom's garden today," Reva admitted. "That was sweet."

"He's courting you," Jessamine sighed. "How romantic."

"I know," Reva admitted. "But I just don't like him in that way."

"You're stuck on Cyber Chad," Jessamine remarked. "You won't even give anyone else a chance."

"Jessamine, shut your mouth," Reva snapped, her face scarlet with embarrassment.

"Reva met some guy named Chad online," Jessamine informed me. "They're both members of a classic film lovers society. They chat all the time. She's pining for him."

"I am not," Reva protested.

"Yes, you are," Jessamine insisted. "You talk to him nearly every night."

"We have a lot in common," Reva explained. "Not many people our age love old movies, too."

"He's not exactly our age."

"I'm 13; He's 15. That's only a two year difference."

"You haven't even met him," Jessamine said. "He could be lying about his age."

"I doubt it," Reva answered. "We're Facebook friends. I've seen his pictures and friends' list. If he's lying, it's an elaborate lie."

"Well, I declare," Jessamine teased. "You're Facebook friends. This sounds serious."

"Honestly, you behave like you're five years old sometimes," Reva laughed good-naturedly.

Part of me felt glad that Reva liked another guy. Why did I care, though? Kevin didn't know I existed, except when he caught me checking him out!

"I just like to tease you," Jessamine assured her.

"And you do it so well," Reva retorted.

Suddenly a commotion broke out on the field. Forest Springs' track team formed a huddle around something, or someone. A few girls began crying while others looked terrified.

Mr. Shears, the track coach, shouted, "Kevin's having a seizure. Someone call 911 and fetch the school nurse!"

Immediately, I jumped to my feet and sprinted toward the nurse's office. I ran so fast that the whizzing wind almost hurt my ears.

Five minutes later, I returned with Nurse Allen. By then Reva and Jessamine had joined the circle.

Barely able to breathe, I stood by myself reciting a silent prayer.

Please, please, please let Kevin be okay. Please let him be okay.

Suddenly Kevin's voice filtered from the crowd.

"I'm fine," he assured people. "Really. I promise."

I walked back to the group. Kevin's usual tanned face looked ashen. Sirens blared as emergency vehicles arrived on the scene.

"Oh geez," he groaned. "An ambulance, really?"

"It's standard protocol," Nurse Allen insisted, grabbing his right wrist and checking his pulse. "Do you have seizures often?"

"Not really," Kevin answered.

"He's an epileptic," said Bryan Raven, his best friend.

Kevin shot him a dirty look.

"Sorry, Bro," Bryan replied. "Your health comes first."

Kevin suffered from epilepsy? How did I never know that?

Ten minutes later, Kevin departed for Forest Springs Memorial Hospital. The crowd slowly dispersed as Mr. Shears declared the track meet officially canceled.

Jessamine clutched my hand tightly and looked at me sympathetically.

"Kevin will be fine," she whispered so Reva couldn't hear. "I know how much he means to you. Don't worry one bit. The doctors

will take great care of him."

I blushed a deep red. How did Jessamine know I liked Kevin? Was I that obvious about it?

Leiko walked over to us. Her face showed concern and disappointment.

"I hope Kevin will be okay," she fretted. "That was scary."

"He'll be fine," Reva assured her.

"Can you believe my first track meet got canceled?" Leiko asked. "I was all warmed up and ready to fly."

"There will be other track meets," Reva replied.

"Yeah, yeah," Leiko grumbled.

"I better get home," I said. "I have homework."

"I want to talk to you," a voice behind me boomed.

I turned around and found myself looking directly into Mr. Shears' firm brown eyes.

"Me?" I asked, confused.

"Yes, you," Mr. Shears answered. "What's your name?"

"Emylee," I answered, my heart rate quickening.

"Your speed is amazing," he said. "I want you on my track team."

Christine Dzidrums

Chat 1

Reva! There u are!

Hi Chad.

I've been searching for u for days!

Whoops. Sorry. I've been really busy.

Saving the world again, huh?

haha That's me...everyone's hero!

Seriously, though. I've missed u.

You have?

Of course! Who else could I tease mercilessly? ;-)

I'm glad to be of use to you. ;-)

Nah, I really have missed u tho'.

OK, now you're embarrassing me.

It's true. I saw Mutiny on the Bounty on Saturday and thought of u.

The Charles Laughton/Clark Gable version?

Of course. I'm no fool.

Clark Gable sigh

Laughton's Captain Bligh is the greatest film villain of all time.

Oh, I agree. Give me his Bligh over Anthony Hopkins' Hannibal Lechter any day of the week.

I love that I can talk to u about classic b/w films. Other girls would give me strange looks if I said names like David O. Selznick or Cecil B. DeMille in front of them.

Cecil B. DeMille? Wasn't he in that vampire movie?

Very funny.

I try. ;-)

So where have u been?

I moved into a new home. It took me awhile to get the Internet hooked up.

Wait. U moved again?

Yes, lucky me.

This is the third time you've moved since I've met u, and I've barely known u a year.

I know.

Why do u move so often? Are you an army brat?

No, I told you already. My mom is a writer, and she likes to live all over the country.

Hmm

Hmm??

I'll bet your mom is a spy!

I think you've seen The Man Who Knew Too Much too many times.

This guy doesn't know very much at all... about u.

Don't be ridiculous. You know a lot about me.

I know your first name is Reva. I know u like classic movies. U have 2 sisters, whose names I don't know. Your favorite book is The Great Gatsby, but u also love Tender is the Night. Your favorite movie is It Happened One Night. Your mom is a writer, but u never talk about your father. U lived in Florida but u never went to Disney World or Sea World or any other tourist trap. U love the ocean, cobb salads and Cherry soda.

See? You could almost write a book on me.

A mystery book.

ha ha Very funny, Smarty Pants.

It stinks. U know a lot about me, but I know very little about u. What's your story?

Are you hoary-eyed?

Am I what????

Hoary-eyed. It means drunk.

Oh yeah. There's one other thing I know about u.

What's that?

U use the strangest expressions sometimes!!!!!!!!!

LOL

I'm always Googling your phrases just so I can understand u.

Sorry. I am a bit weird sometimes.

You're not weird. You're just very...unique.

Uh, thanks, I think?

You're welcome. I mean it as a compliment. You're unlike any girl I've ever met. It's almost like...

Like what?

Like you're from another era.

Sorry, Chad. I need to go. My sister wants to use the computer now.

But we've barely talked at all.

Sorry, but she has a homework assignment to finish. Talk to you later.

Grrr. Fine. Later, Mystery Girl.

Chapter 8
"Honor"

And that's how Coach Shears recruited me onto Forest Springs' track team. Of course, I refused at first. Number one, organized sports aren't my thing. Number two, I felt anxious about having teammates. Nevertheless, in the end, thanks to the Fay sisters' encouragement, I joined the team.

Of course it wouldn't exactly be horrible seeing Kevin at practice every day. Meanwhile, news of his seizure had spread throughout school. Guys spent the next day making ambulance sirens at him, while girls approached him with big doe eyes expressing their concern. Kevin seemed uncomfortable with the attention, often grimacing under the bright spotlight. I think he wished everyone would just forget the incident entirely.

At my first practice, Kevin sat next to me during stretches. I nearly lost my lunch when his tanned arm brushed against mine.

"I, uh," Kevin began, clearing his throat. "Thank you for getting the school nurse yesterday. I heard you fetched her."

"No problem," I answered. "I would have done it for anyone."

Now why did I say that? It totally sounded like he wasn't anyone special. Not that I wanted him to know that I thought he was special but…

"Well," Kevin smiled. "It was still cool of you."

Sigh. Did he actually smile at me? Me? Boring, invisible Emma? He had the best smile. Double sigh

"Are you feeling better?" I asked, hoping he wouldn't notice my flushed cheeks.

"Yeah, I'm totally fine," he smiled sheepishly. "It wasn't a big deal."

"I'm glad," I replied.

Was this truly happening? I was carrying on a conversation with Kevin Briggs. No doubt it ranked as the ultimate highlight of my short, lousy life.

Just then, Leiko sat beside us with a groan.

"Coach Shears wants me to run cross country," she grumbled.

"Cross country is awesome," Kevin exclaimed. "It's probably the hardest event."

"I don't want anything hard," Leiko complained. "I'm just trying to avoid P.E. class."

"Shears wouldn't put you in cross country unless he had serious faith in you," Kevin said. "He looks for athletes in phenomenal shape and with great stamina."

"Whatevs," Leiko replied. "I'll do it but I'm not happy."

Just then Coach Shears clapped his hands and called a team meeting. My heart soared as Kevin moved even closer to me.

"Listen up," Coach Shears said. "Melissa Kelly has the chicken pox. If you haven't had it, you will probably get it."

I caught the chicken pox in first grade. Grandma made me a different soup every day. She also bought me popsicles. I ate one each night until I'd polished off the box.

"Also, because Melissa is out for several weeks, she can't make the brownies for tomorrow's bake sale," he continued. "So who wants to volunteer?"

Suddenly, Kevin's arm shot up. He sported a devilish grin.

"Are you volunteering, Briggs?" Coach Shears asked.

"Of course not," Kevin answered, as some people giggled.

"I think our new teammates should receive the honor of baking brownies," he announced, pointing to Leiko and me.

"You little sneak," Leiko gasped.

"I second that motion," Bryan grinned.

"Sounds good to me," Coach replied. "Leiko and Emylee, we need 50 brownies by lunchtime tomorrow."

Unreal. What was happening? First I be-

came friends with the Fay sisters. Then I got recruited for the track team. Now I'm baking brownies for a bake sale? Who exchanged my solitary existence for the life of a social butterfly?

"Let's make the brownies at your house," an annoyed Leiko told me.

Absolutely not. No way would she enter my crummy house and risk meeting Mom. That's where I drew the line.

"Can we bake them at your house?" I asked. "My mother has company tonight."

Leiko shrugged and glared at Kevin. He waved mockingly in response.

"Fine, whatevs," she answered.

So I would see where the Fay sisters lived. And I'd meet their mother, too. I admittedly felt very curious about their home life.

I turned to ask Leiko if she had brownie ingredients at home. She wasn't looking at me, though. Instead, she gazed at Kevin, who now chatted with Bryan. Only Leiko didn't appear angry or bothered anymore. Instead she smiled faintly, like she enjoyed his attention.

Could it be? Oh great. Leiko also liked Kevin Briggs.

Chat 2

Hey Stranger.

Hi Chad.

U left so quickly yesterday. Everything ok?

Everything's great.

Glad to hear it. So I watched Animal Crackers last night.

Good choice. That's probably my favorite Marx Brothers movie.

One morning I shot an elephant in my pajamas.

How did he get in your pajamas?

LOL

:-)

Are we ever going to meet?

Wow, that was an abrupt topic change.

I know. I just thought I'd ask. ;-)

Meeting wouldn't be a good idea.

Why?

It's complicated.

Look, Reva. If this is about something superficial like your looks, get over it. I don't care what u look like. U will always be beautiful to me. I've connected with u in a way that I've never connected with anyone.

Same here.

Then what gives? Why can't we meet?

Because it's not a good idea.

Reva, is it because...

?

Are you worried about what I look like? I'm no Rudolph Valentino but I'm ok looking. I don't think I'd scare anyone in a dark alley. ;-)

Chad, no... Your looks aren't important to me.

Great. So let's meet!

First of all, you live all the way in California, and I'm in New England.

So you're living in New England now? Well, there's something I didn't know.

Yes. I'm nearly 3000 miles away. Too far. Besides, a 13-year-old shouldn't jet to California to meet some guy she met online.

But I'm not "some guy." U know that. We're geeky film buffs. ;-) Our friendship is purely innocent.

I know, I know.

So let me come to u.

Be serious.

Well why not? Let me take all the risk. Where in New England do u live? I'll fly out to see u one weekend.

You're 15. You're just going to fly cross-country by yourself?

Get a grip, Reva. I'm not a kid. I have flown alone before.

Plane tickets are expensive.

They can be, but I'm a whiz at finding deals. Besides I have money in my savings account. I'll happily dip into it if it means I get to meet u.

You'd do that just for me?

In a New York minute.

You're crazy.

About u. Come on, what do u say? We'll meet somewhere public, like a coffee shop. U can bring your sisters with u if it makes you more comfortable.

Why is it so important to you that we meet?

Why is it so important to u that we don't meet?

My life is very complicated.

You're 13. How complicated can it be?

You really have no clue.

So tell me. U already know my life story.

I know that your mom and dad are divorced and you live with your dad. I know you've read Catcher in the Rye 8 times, watched Treasure of Sierra Madre 14 times and you can't stand your 5th period English teacher. That's all I know.

Ask me anything.

I can't do this, Chad. Our friendship is starting to get too complicated.

It's already complicated. Admit that u like me.

I do like you.

I knew it. :-)

And it terrifies me.

Why?

I can't get into it right now. It's not a good time.

Reva, it's never a good time for u.

I have to get started on my Algebra homework. I'll chat with you later.

Yeah, yeah. Later.

Chapter 9
The Fay Home

"That was really rotten of Kevin," Leiko remarked as we headed north toward the Fay home.

Except Leiko grinned, like she enjoyed being teased by Kevin.

Seriously? Leiko liked Kevin? When? Why? Shouldn't she be crushing on some guy with purple hair and a nose ring? Why did she like clean-cut Kevin?

Because he's gorgeous. And funny. And smart. And athletic. And sweet. And likable. And a bully crusher. And absolutely perfect.

Why wouldn't Leiko like him? Just because she has blue hair and scowls a lot doesn't mean she's blind and dumb. Of course she would find Kevin attractive. Who wouldn't? Well, besides Reva.

I shook my head as we crossed a busy intersection. Whether it was Reva rejecting the school's most eligible guy, Jessamine befriend-

ing me, or Leiko baking brownies, the three sisters always surprised me.

"Learn to drive, Moron," Leiko shouted at a motorist who plowed through a red light just as we jumped safely onto the curb.

The burly, bald driver extended his hand out the window and offered an obscene gesture.

"I should put a spell on you," Leiko screamed.

"A spell?" I laughed.

"Honestly," she sputtered, readjusting the backpack on her tiny shoulders. "Forest Springs' drivers are horrible. That jerk could have killed you…us."

"Our town is notorious for lousy drivers," I replied. "People build up serious road rage living in such a confined space."

"I'm surprised there aren't more traffic deaths here," she said.

"There have been several fatality accidents already this year," I told her.

"Be careful," she warned. "You just can't trust anyone nowadays…especially people driving a big metal machine with wheels."

"This walking stinks anyway," she continued. "I hate walking like some mortal."

I giggled at Leiko's melodramatic nature. She cracked me up sometimes.

"I hate to break it to you but we're all mortals, whether we like it or not," I said.

Leiko muttered something under her breath, but I couldn't hear what she said.

"Well, anyway," she replied. "I hate walking. I wish there was an easier way to get around."

On that last remark, her mouth twitched several times. It was like she enjoyed a private joke.

"Well I left my Porsche at home today," I quipped.

"And I forgot my fairy wings," Leiko shot back, laughing especially hard.

By then we had passed uptown, where traffic became sparse because Forest Springs' woods began. Leiko headed straight into a thick area crowded with trees and bushes.

"Where are you going?" I asked, following reluctantly.

"Home," she answered, pushing past a wild tree branch and stepping through fallen leaves.

"You live in the woods?" I asked.

"No," Leiko stressed. "I live in a house in the woods."

In my 12 years as a Forest Springs resident I'd never ventured into the woods. Old legend claimed that in the 1920s, two high-school boys died in the woods after becoming lost during a severe snowstorm.

When I was a first grader, my teacher's brother, John Witt, insisted the woods were haunted. The then high schooler claimed that he and Bobby Olsen entered the woods on a dare and were chased away by two teenage ghosts who warned them never to re-enter, or they would die a young death. For several years afterwards, I got chills whenever anyone mentioned the woods.

Though I no longer believed in supernatural or mythical creatures, I still got the creeps thinking about the woods. Leave it to the Fay sisters to actually live there.

I obviously dragged my feet too much, because Leiko stopped in her tracks and delivered an exaggerated sigh.

"I've seen you run," she said accusingly. "You're not slow. Speed it up. I promise that no ghost or animal or demon will get you."

Leiko continued marching through the woods. I had no choice but to follow her. A few moments later, she stopped again.

"We're here," she announced.

Before me sat an adorable home that looked a fairy tale dwelling. A beautiful pink cottage with a royal blue gabled roof was surrounded by a perfectly-manicured lawn and a white picket fence.

"Is this for real?" I asked Leiko.

"It is a bit decadent," she admitted, opening a tiny gate.

We walked up a cobblestone path lined with yellow and violet pansies that led to a wrap-around porch outfitted with white wicker furniture. It was so perfect I could picture the Fay sisters spending a lovely summer evening on it enjoying the fresh outdoors.

"How have I lived in Forest Springs my entire life and never seen this house?" I asked incredulously.

"It was abandoned," Leiko explained. "Our lead.... uh....my mom hired some guys to fix it up."

The Fay sisters were surely loaded. There was no way ordinary workers restored the home. It looked absolutely stunning.

When we entered the house, a perfume of fresh flowers greeted us.

"What's that scent?" I asked Leiko. "It's wonderful"

"Sweet Pea flowers," she answered. "Jessamine went overboard with potpourri."

I made a mental note to buy Sweet Pea fragrance the next time I went into town. I wondered if Kevin had ever smelled the scent and if he would like it.

Hardwood floors shined so brightly, they glittered. Oak furniture appeared freshly polished and carved with floral designs. Delicate lace curtains hung from spotless windows. There were no signs of dust bunnies or smudges or clutter. The home resembled a perfect little dollhouse.

"I can't believe you actually live here," I said with admiration. "This looks like a home in an architectural magazine. I've never seen anything more gorgeous in my entire life."

"Thanks," Leiko said, tossing her backpack on the floor. "Jessamine is an interior design nut, and Reva is a neat freak. Thanks to their combined obsessions, we have a nice house."

Blood rushed to my cheeks as I realized that Leiko and Reva had seen my dumpy house, the outside of it anyway.

Suddenly I spotted a gorgeous antique

wooden box with intricate etching. I walked over to inspect its perfect craftsmanship. Three knobs and a counter sat at its bottom.

"That's an Atwater Kent," Leiko revealed. "It's an old radio from the 1920s."

"It's beautiful."

"It's Reva's baby," Leiko answered. "She's owned it for many years."

Just then a stunning brunette in her mid-30s entered the room. She wore a long, sweeping lavender skirt with an ivy silk blouse.

"You must be Emylee," she announced, extending her hand. "The girls have told me so many wonderful things about you."

"Nice to meet you," I replied, shaking her warm hand.

Could this family be any more perfect?

"Please call me Odessa," she smiled.

"Hi, Odessa," I replied uncomfortably.

"I've wanted to meet you," she continued. "I wanted to thank you personally."

"Thank me?" I asked surprised. "For what?"

"For taking my daughters under your wing when they were new girls at an unfamiliar school," she answered.

Was she kidding? I helped the perfect Fay sisters? Plain little me?

"They were so grateful for your friendship," she continued.

"I'm grateful for their friendship as well," I replied.

"May I get you something to drink?" Odessa asked. "Would you like a glass of lemonade? Iced tea, perhaps? I made both beverages this afternoon since I wasn't sure which one you might prefer."

"How did you know I was coming over today?" I asked in confusion.

Odessa froze for a few seconds, maintaining her fixed smile while she considered my question. Finally, Leiko spoke.

"I texted her after Kevin volunteered us," she explained.

The muscles in Odessa's perfect smile relaxed upon hearing Leiko's explanation.

"My daughters and I are avid texters," she said lightly. "We're attached to our cell phones. You've discovered our embarrassing family secret."

I smiled and decided that I liked Odessa. Like Jessamine, she seemed calming and approachable, despite her ravishing beauty. If I could pick my own mother, I would want someone like her.

"So may I offer you a beverage?" Odessa asked again. "You girls must be parched after an afternoon on the track."

Though I had downed water after practice, I still felt thirsty. My first day had wiped me out.

"Sure," I replied. "Any drink would be fine. Thank you."

"I'll get it," Leiko said. "So, uh, Mom, don't you have a business meeting to attend?"

Leiko seemed anxious for her mother

to leave. That surprised me. If I had a mom as beautiful, successful and kind as Odessa, I would show her off, not try to hide her.

"You're right," Odessa responded quickly, as if she had just remembered an urgent matter.

"Emylee," she smiled again. "Would you please excuse me? I have to meet a colleague."

"Of course," I replied.

Moments later I stood in an immaculate kitchen, holding a chilled glass of lemonade while Leiko scrounged through a cupboard.

"Surely we have brownie mix in here somewhere," she grumbled impatiently.

"Is there something I can help you find?" Reva asked, entering the room.

"Hello, Emylee," she added.

"Don't worry," Leiko told her. "I won't destroy your pristine kitchen. I'm just searching for brownie mix."

"Why?" Reva asked. "You never bake."

"Long story, short," Leiko called over her shoulder. "Track team. Bake sale. Emylee and I were thrown under a bus. Brownies. Mix. Now."

"Don't make brownies from a mix," Reva said, her voice thick with disapproval. "They're much tastier from scratch."

"That takes too long," Leiko replied dismissively.

She then accidentally knocked some boxes from the cupboard. They tumbled to the floor.

"Step away from the kitchen, Leiko," Reva commanded. "Emylee and I will make the brownies."

Leiko brushed her hair out of her eyes. She looked pleased by her sister's offer.

"That would be terrific. Thanks. You're the best."

"Mmm hmmm," Reva said, picking up Leiko's mess. "Start your homework. Leave the baking to us."

"You don't have to ask me twice," Leiko chirped, heading for the living room. "I am outta here."

"Looks like we're making brownies," Reva smiled.

83

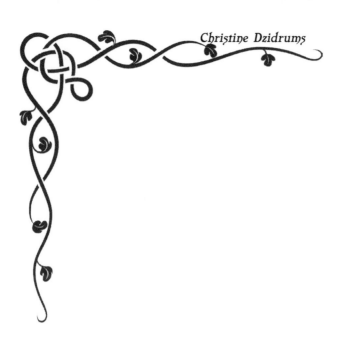

Christine Dzidrums

Chapter 10
Confessions

I didn't really make brownies so much as I spent the next hour watching Reva zip around the kitchen like a gourmet chef. Even the way she stirred ingredients and poured them into a baking dish seemed elegant.

"How was your first day of track?" she asked.

"Not as bad as I thought," I answered honestly.

"You thought it would go badly?" she asked confused.

Of course, Reva never dreaded social situations. With her good looks and cool confidence, mingling with classmates came naturally to her. Meanwhile, I agonized over every interaction and then replayed conversations in my mind, convinced that I had made a fool of myself.

"I'm not the greatest conversationalist," I replied.

"I think you hold conversations quite well," she said, stirring a fresh brownie batch.

"I'm not like you and your sisters," I said. "I lack your confidence."

"Do you think I wasn't frightened my first day at Forest Springs?" Reva asked. "I was petrified. We all were."

"No way," I replied in disbelief.

"Yes way," she answered. "It's intimidating walking into a new school while everyone stares and forms instant opinions of you."

"I hadn't thought of it that way," I admitted. "You Fay sisters seem so composed."

"We're very good actors," Reva assured me. "Trust me. It wasn't easy for any of us."

She poured the batter into a glass dish and wiped her hands on a napkin.

"Take me, for instance," she continued. "I stop talking when I'm nervous."

"I hadn't noticed," I answered honestly.

Reva placed the brownie pan in the oven, adjusted the temperature and set a timer. Then she returned to the table and sat down.

"You don't talk much yourself," she commented.

"I don't have a lot to say," I shrugged.

"Is your mom a big talker?" she asked.

"I guess."

"What's she like?"

"She has many friends," I replied, actually telling the truth.

"But what is she like?" Reva pushed.

"She's a good mother," I lied. "She works all the time."

Reva stared at me thoughtfully for a long time. I tried not to squirm under her intense gaze.

"So you don't have any other relatives anywhere?" she asked.

"Not since my grandmother died a few years ago."

"It sounds like you were close to her," Reva said softly.

My throat tightened. Buried emotions threatened to break me down. I felt scared to speak, so I nodded instead.

Reva waited for me to speak.

"We were this close," I said, holding up two fingers side by side. "She was my best friend."

"And what was she like?" Reva asked.

I shut my eyes and thought of Grandma. Happy memories flooded my mind.

"Warm. Kind. Loving," I answered. "She smelled like apple spice and gave the best hugs ever. Her eyes truly twinkled. She always repeated the same corny jokes. Then when she reached the punch line, she would laugh as if she were hearing it for the first time."

Reva rested her right elbow on the table and cradled her chin with her hand.

"She had the best laugh," I continued. "It

was contagious…a laugh that made you smile just hearing it."

"I wish I could have met her," Reva said.

"You would have loved her," I smiled.

"No doubt," she replied.

As I thought about Grandma's laughter, a small tear rolled down my cheek. I wiped it away, embarrassed.

"Have you ever loved anyone else like that?" Reva asked gingerly.

I thought about her question honestly.

"Not human," I answered.

"What do you mean?" Reva asked, sounding alarmed.

"I owned a dog once," I admitted reluctantly. "I only had him for two weeks, but I loved him so much."

"Oh, a dog," Reva said, thick relief in her voice. "I've never owned a pet, but it must be easy to love a helpless animal."

"I was nine years old, and Grandma had just died" I told her. "He was a stray - a Lancashire Heeler. I discovered his breed from a dog website. His coat was so filthy that it looked dead. His rib cage stuck out from lack of nourishment. When our eyes met, my heart melted, but I resisted bringing him into my home at first."

"How come?" Reva asked.

I couldn't tell the truth. That I could barely care for myself, how could I have nurtured an animal?

"I was afraid my mother wouldn't let me keep him," I fibbed.

"That's understandable," Reva replied.

"So I left him food scraps outside our front door," I continued. "I cried watching him eat the first meal I left for him. He devoured it like it might disappear. After a while, he began sleeping on our porch, so I placed a warm blanket outside for him. Then every day when I walked home from school, he waited for me with his tail wagging like I was the world's most important person."

I began crying softly, but for some reason, I kept talking. I wanted to spill out my guts to Reva.

"He was the only one in the world who noticed me...loved me...and I loved him, too. Eventually I brought him into my home. Mom put up a small fuss at first but she quickly got over it. I named him Jake. For two weeks, he was my entire life and I was his. It was the happiest I'd felt since Grandma died."

I took a deep breath. Heavy shudders emanated from me. Reva grabbed my hand and gripped it tightly.

"Then one day I came home from school and Jake wasn't waiting for me. I walked the neighborhood every day calling out to him, but I never saw him again. I cried myself to sleep every night for weeks. I'd like to think someone gave him a good home and loved him just as much as I had. I wanted to believe he was in a warm home...happy and eating until his stomach swelled."

The tears gushed. I swiped them away, but they kept reappearing. I pulled my hand away from Reva. Suddenly, I felt horrified by my emotional breakdown.

"You don't have to be embarrassed," Reva

assured me. "It's okay to talk about your feelings. I'm here for you. You need a friend."

"I don't need anyone," I snapped, standing up. "I don't need you, your sisters, the track team or my mom. I have done just fine by myself."

"Please," Reva pleaded. "Let us help you."

I heard something awful in her tone...something horribly embarrassing. Pity.

"I don't need your help," I yelled. "Just leave me alone. All of you. Butt out of my life."

Sensing someone had entered the room, I whirled around. Leiko stood watching our interaction. For once the mouthy teen looked speechless...her mouth agape. I ran for the door.

"Please don't leave," Reva begged. "Let me make you some hot tea. Calm down first, okay?"

"Leave me alone!" I shouted.

"Do you want the truth?" I asked. "My mother never wanted me and she definitely doesn't love me. She has spent her life ignoring the biggest mistake she made...me. She thinks if she ignores me long enough, I'll eventually go away. Do you know how it feels to know that your own mother doesn't love you? Do you know what it's like to care for yourself since you were just a kid? To live your entire life as a lie?"

"I know more than you can ever imagine," Reva replied, tears piling up in her eyes.

"Oh really?" I laughed. "You can to relate me? You with your perfect looks? You with your gorgeous sisters and your stunning moth-

er? You who lives in an ideal home? You with your superior IQ? You who has won the heart of Kevin Briggs, the only person I ever hoped would notice me."

"Things aren't always as they appear," Reva said quietly. "If you would only listen."

"I don't want to listen," I screamed. "I'm tired of listening. I've spent my entire life as a silent observer."

"Just let her go," Leiko said softly, almost sympathetically.

And with those words, I bolted out the front door.

I raced through the woods. Partly because I feared being alone in the wilderness, partly because I yearned to escape the uncovered memories.

Just as I neared the clearing, I ran smack into Jessamine, who wore a perfectly pressed cheerleading outfit.

"Emylee," she exclaimed, placing her hands on my shoulders. "What's going on?"

"Leave me alone," I shouted as I shoved her away and continued running.

I sped through uptown, dodging red lights. I ran past Forest Springs Middle School and Yeoman's Grocery Store, where Mom worked when she wasn't plastered. I never slowed down, even when I hit the town's rural area. I sprung past farms and rundown homes and over railroad tracks.

Cars probably honked. People likely hollered at me. I can't remember.

I only heard my heavy gasps as I sprinted

toward home. Suddenly, it started raining. The ground turned muddy and perilous. I didn't stop running, though. I sprinted up the familiar hill near my house. As I neared the crest, a pickup truck flew over the top, veering recklessly out of control and headed right at me. I kept running, though, even when I heard screeching brakes and my own voice screaming for my life.

Chapter 11
Transformation

The days following the accident were a haze. I slept for over 80 hours, while Jessamine, Reva and Leiko took turns observing me.

During this time I experienced crazy dreams. I soared over the Grand Canyon with the lightness of a sparrow. I helped a nightingale rediscover her voice. I even nursed a colt back to health and returned him to his grateful mother.

Then on Saturday afternoon, just as the sisters feared my transformation had gone awfully wrong, I stirred. Though I'd spent three days unconscious, I awoke with a remarkable lightness. My cumbersome emotional baggage? Gone! The internal pain and sadness? It felt like someone else's memory.

"What's going on?" I asked, sitting up in bed.

The Fay sisters stood watching me apprehensively.

"You're one of us now," Leiko replied flatly.

"One of you?" I blinked, wondering if I was dreaming again.

What did she mean? I would never be like the Fay girls.

I nearly laughed at her absurd comment. No way did plain me resemble the extraordinary sisters.

"What do you mean I'm one of you now?" I repeated.

Jessamine walked over to me. She clasped and unclasped her perfectly manicured hands and ran them anxiously through her silky hair.

"There's so much to explain," she said. "Let's discuss this when you're more lucid."

"Discuss what?" I demanded.

Jessamine glanced hesitantly at Reva, who nodded in response.

"Go ahead," she said. "I think that she will handle the news just fine."

"What news?" I asked.

I felt really freaked. My legs turned to jelly. I sensed the sisters might reveal life-altering news.

Jessamine closed her eyes. Then she inhaled and exhaled deeply. It felt like hours before she spoke.

"What's the last thing you remember?" Jessamine asked gently.

I couldn't recall anything. My head felt foggy. I stared blankly at the girls.

"We baked brownies," Reva said. "You became upset and left in a huff. It began pouring. You were running home when..."

94   "A red pickup truck came over the hill..." I remembered.

I closed my eyes, visualizing the scene. Suddenly, the memories came barreling back.

"It was going way too fast and lost control," I recalled. "It flew right at me and…"

"And I saved you," Jessamine finished quietly.

"You saved me?" I echoed. "That's impossible. You weren't on that road."

"I saved you," she repeated calmly.

"But how?" I asked. "I was alone."

"I was there," she answered. "You just didn't see me."

"You were there?" I repeated slowly. "I didn't see you? What do you mean?"

"Were you invisible?" I laughed. "Do you have special powers?"

Dead air flooded the room. None of the girls spoke for a long time. Finally, Reva broke the silence.

"Emylee, please listen carefully," she said. "This revelation may be difficult for you to believe, but it's true."

"I'm listening," I answered.

"Jessamine, Leiko and I are fairies," she revealed.

I laughed. It was a loud, awkward laugh that hung in the air for an eternity. No one else, however, laughed.

This was an early April Fool's prank. They were joking. After all, why else would brilliant, levelheaded Reva tell such a ridiculous story?

A million questions floated through my head, but I just stared blankly at the Fay sisters. They looked back solemnly.

"Fairies," I finally repeated.

Reva nodded, while Jessamine smiled meekly. Leiko, meanwhile, looked annoyed and almost angry.

"You mean like Tinkerbelle?" I asked.

"Do I look like Tinkerbelle?" an annoyed Leiko asked.

"Well, you don't exactly look like a fairy," I answered.

"And what do fairies look like?" Reva asked.

"They…well…they're tiny," I sputtered. "They're pixies…or at least they would be if…"

"If what?" Reva prodded.

"If they existed," I answered.

"I've got news for you," Leiko rolled her eyes. "I'm a fairy. Jessamine is a fairy. Reva is a fairy. We're not pixies. We're real. We exist…just like you do."

"And no," she added. "We don't leave money under your pillow every time you lose a tooth."

"Okay," I said, swallowing hard. "Suppose you're telling the truth and you are fairies… Why are you in Forest Springs?"

"Where should we be?" Leiko asked. "Neverland?"

I shrugged weakly.

"Neverland doesn't exist," Leiko said. "But we do."

"We're altruistic beings," Reva explained. "We travel the world helping people in need."

"Wait," I shook my head dubiously. "I'm some rescue case?"

"You were," Leiko answered. "Until Jessamine destroyed everything."

"I did the best I could," she protested.

"But she saved my life," I said. "How did she ruin everything? I don't understand."

"I saved your life because I wasn't able to save you," Jessamine answered.

"Are you trying to confuse me?" I asked. "Because I feel like you're all speaking a foreign language. I don't understand anything you're saying."

"Our mission, our sole reason for existence, is to save children who are in danger of being forgotten forever," Reva explained.

"I'm a forgotten child," I said calmly.

"I'm afraid so," Reva replied sympathetically.

"What happens to forgotten children?" I asked, dreading the answer.

The sisters exchanged a knowing look. Finally, Reva spoke.

"Those who aren't saved, when they leave this world, fall into the ablitero," she answered.

"Ab what?" I asked.

"Ablitero is the place between earth and heaven," Leiko answered. "It's where unclaimed souls stay for eternity."

"Unclaimed?"

"People that no one will miss when they die," Jessamine explained delicately.

"And I'm a person that no one would miss," I finished.

"If Jessamine had let that truck squash you to bits, you would have booked a one way ticket to ablitero," Leiko stated.

"Our job, that we failed to complete in time, was to find you a family on earth," Jessamine explained apologetically. "We were trying to help you. We were trying to find someone to love you so that when the time came, you wouldn't fall into the ablitero, but we misjudged the time we had. Suddenly the truck was coming at you, and I had two choices... let the car hit you and you'd be stuck in ablitero forever...or save you by turning you into a fairy."

"Wait...what?" I asked.

Jessamine, Reva and Leiko exchanged anxious looks and then looked back at me.

"Wait just a second," I said. "Are you saying that I'm now...a fairy?"

Chapter 12
Revelations

"Yes," Reva replied seriously. "You're a fairy now."

"So you just snapped your fingers and suddenly I'm a fairy?" I asked in amazement and disbelief.

"It wasn't that simple," she answered. "You slept for over three days while the transformation took place."

I looked at myself critically. My hair suffered serious bedhead. I still sported the beat-up shorts that I'd worn to track practice. My blouse had a large purple stain from when I spilled grape juice on it at lunch. My worn socks had a hole where my big toe peaked out. I examined the picture perfect trio and burst out laughing at the contrast. I sure as heck didn't look like a beautiful fairy.

"She's lost it," Leiko said, shaking her head.

"I'm not fairy material," I said, after I'd stopped laughing.

"You can say that again," Leiko snorted.

"Quiet, Leiko," Jessamine scolded before smiling reassuringly at me.

"All in due time," Reva answered.

"Where are my wings?" I asked, straining to look at my back.

"You have to earn those," Reva replied.

"Where are your wings?" I asked the sisters.

"They only appear when we need them," Jessamine explained.

"Can you fly?" I asked.

"Of course," Reva answered.

"Can I fly?" I asked.

"You will earn that privilege once you've completed your studies," she said.

"My studies?"

"Your fairy powers aren't just handed to you," Jessamine explained. "You have to work for them…just as we did."

"You have magical powers?"

"Yes," Reva replied. "We all possess a unique gift."

"What's yours?"

"I can persuade anyone to reveal his or her thoughts," she said.

"That's why I so easily opened up to you about Grandma and Jake," I responded.

"Yes," she admitted.

"And what's your special power?" I asked Jessamine.

"I can read a person's heart," she revealed.

"That's why you knew I liked..." I stopped myself from finishing the sentence.

Jessamine nodded.

"And I can uncover an object or person's past just by touching it," Leiko announced before I asked.

"Which is why you bought that striped blouse at Second Chance," I finished. "You knew it had been someone's lucky shirt."

"Bingo," she answered.

"We all have unique powers," Reva explained. "But we try to use them sparingly."

"Why?"

"Humans mustn't see them," she explained. "We maintain a low profile, so we blend with mortals."

"Mortals?" I asked. "You mean..."

"We're suspended in time," Jessamine explained. "We don't ever age...and neither will you."

"Ever?" I asked.

"Congratulations," Leiko said. "You'll be experiencing puberty for all eternity."

"So fairies can't die?"

"Well...." Reva hedged. "It's complicated. We'll get into details later."

"Prove it," I said.

Reva wrinkled her brow, while Jessamine and Leiko stared quizzically.

"Prove what?" Reva asked.

"Prove that you're fairies...that I'm a fairy," I said. "I'm sorry but this sounds absolutely insane. I need proof."

Jessamine looked uncertainly at Reva. Her sister nodded.

"Okay," Jessamine said. "I'll prove that we're fairies."

I felt fear and excitement combined.

"Summon a happy memory," she told me. "Don't tell me what you're thinking. Recall the happiest time of your life."

I started to shut my eyes when Jessamine pulled a silver wand adorned with ruby jewels from her sleeve.

"You actually use wands?" I asked incredulously.

"Mmm hmmm," she answered. "When it's absolutely necessary. Now think of a good memory."

Of course, I thought of Jake. Jessamine closed her eyes and nodded as if I'd told her my memory. I watched her dubiously. How could she possibly know my thoughts?

Jessamine murmured some phrases in a foreign language. Then her wand glowed radiantly and filled the room with warmth.

Suddenly I heard the faint clinking of an ID tag hitting a collar followed by the pattering of dog feet. Before I knew it, Jake ran into the room. When my old friend spotted me, he leaped into my arms and licked me joyously.

"Jake," I whispered emotionally.

"How did you...?" I asked Jessamine in astonishment.

Jake showered me with wet kisses as tears poured down my cheeks.

"I have the gift of reading a person's heart," Jessamine reminded me.

At that moment, I didn't want to think about special powers or fairies or wands. I only cared about Jake. I clutched him tightly and buried my face in his fur.

"Can... Can I keep him?" I asked, my voice hoarse with emotion.

"Call it a welcome to the family gift," Reva smiled.

"Welcome home, Jake," I cooed, nuzzling him.

"Well?" a pleased Jessamine asked.

"I do believe in fairies," I answered.

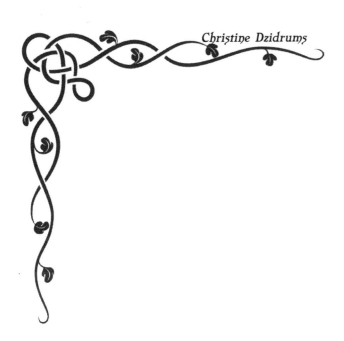

Christine Dzidrums

Chapter 13
Fair Youth

I showered the Fays with endless questions. They reacted patiently to my unbridled curiosity.

"How long have you been fairies?" I asked.

"I became a fairy in 1880," Jessamine divulged. "Of us Fay girls, I've lived the fairy life the longest."

"That's why you carry such class and elegance," I replied.

"I've likely maintained the finer manners I learned over a century ago," Jessamine blushed.

"1928," Reva revealed. "That's when I metamorphosed into a fairy."

"Of course," I snapped my fingers. "Your hairdo, the quirky expressions. It all makes sense now."

"I miss those days," Reva reflected wistfully. "People were happier back then."

"The year was 1978," Leiko pro-

claimed. "I surrendered mortality about the time punk became a cultural phenomenon."

"I bought the Ramones debut record," she continued. "I loved The Clash and Blondie when they were just entering the scene. Now they're vintage bands."

"Vinyl," she sighed. "I miss long play albums."

"How did you become fairies?" I prodded.

"I was a forgotten child heading toward ablitero," Jessamine explained. "Someone saved me and turned me into a fairy."

"Who?"

The girls grew tense. Jessamine appeared flushed as she considered my question.

"Her name was Julissa," she finally answered. "We will tell you about her one day."

"And Odessa saved me," Reva said quickly. "And in turn, I saved Leiko."

"If you can turn anyone into a fairy, why does ablitero even exist?" I asked. "Why not just turn all forgotten children into fairies and avoid ablitero forever?"

"Each of us can only transform a mortal once," Jessamine clarified. "You were my one and only transformation."

Her revelation overwhelmed me. Of all the mortals she had encountered over the years, she chose me. How could I not feel an enormous burden not to let her down?

"Have you saved anyone, Leiko?"

"No," she replied curtly. "I've not yet used that power. I don't want to waste it on just anyone."

She emphasized that last word strongly. If I hadn't already sensed that she disagreed with Jessamine's decision to transform me, I definitely knew it now.

"How did you find me?" I asked, ignoring Leiko's dig.

"Odessa is our fairy troop leader. She assigns us our missions," Jessamine explained. "She sent us here to Forest Springs. She knew you needed our help."

"How?"

"That's her special gift," Reva said. "She's able to locate troubled, endangered souls. Then we travel to their location and attempt to help them."

"So Odessa's not really your mother?" I asked.

"No," Reva said, shaking her head. "Although she's a parental figure that we admire. We tell people she's our mother so no one gets suspicious about a trio of young girls living by themselves. Odessa makes occasional appearances to maintain the charade. She doesn't really live with us full-time. She manages other troops as well."

"There are other fairy troops?" I asked.

"More than you can ever imagine," Leiko answered. "But we're the coolest troop."

"Not that we're biased," Jessamine laughed.

"Will I meet the other troops?" I asked.

"Someday," Reva replied.

"Does your troop have a name?"

"We're named Fair Youth," Leiko announced.

"Fair Youth," I repeated. "I like it."

I still had the most important question left. Though I didn't know the answer, I feared it.

"What becomes of me?" I blurted out. "The mortal me? What will people think when I suddenly disappear from Forest Springs?"

The sisters exchanged anxious glances. No one spoke for a long time. Finally, Reva took my hand.

"You no longer exist," she told me softly. "The second Jessamine snatched you from death and turned you into a fairy, your former life vanished. Your mom won't remember you, nor will your classmates. It's as if you were never born. No one will mourn you because they won't remember you."

It seemed eerily appropriate...me not ever existing. The revelation left me numb.

"Okay," I replied. "I understand."

Throughout the entire conversation, Leiko rarely spoke. She seemed angry, almost bitter. Feeling bolder than I'd ever felt, I confronted her.

"Leiko," I began. "You seem upset. Why?"

Leiko's lips formed a thin straight line. She opened her mouth to speak and promptly shut it. Finally, she finally expressed her thoughts.

"I think you'll be a liability," she stated.

"Leiko, watch your manners," Jessamine scolded. "That's no way to welcome Emylee into our family."

"It's okay," I nodded. "I have always appreciated Leiko's honesty. I'd like to hear her out."

"We've thrived as a trio for decades," she continued. "We don't need another sister, especially someone so reserved, shy and vulnerable."

"Or maybe what you perceive as Emylee's weaknesses might actually be assets," Reva suggested.

Leiko mulled over her sister's remark. Then she shrugged dismissively.

"It's my belief that Emylee lacks the qualities that make a great fairy," she shrugged.

"We won't know anything concrete until she begins her studies," Jessamine pointed out.

"What exactly are my studies?" I asked.

"You'll receive study materials that will guide you toward becoming an official fairy," Reva explained. "You will memorize our guidelines frontwards and backwards. Throughout your lessons, which will take years to complete, you will undergo numerous tests and challenges in preparation for your new role."

I gulped, hoping they didn't see how overwhelmed and frightened I felt.

"I don't think you can handle it," Leiko

said, placing her hands defiantly on her hips. "Prove me wrong."

"When do I start?" I asked.

Chapter 14
A New Beginning

The day after the sisters' revelation, I nursed a horrible headache. I hadn't slept the previous night, tosssing and turning with anxiety and excitement over my new life. Later that morning, Odessa arrived with an important announcement.

"A 13-year-old Iowa girl needs help," she reported. "Prepare for your next mission immediately."

Then my new troop leader walked over to me. She placed her hands on my shoulders and kissed my cheek.

"Welcome to Fair Youth," Odessa smiled. "We anticipate wonderful things from you."

We spent the weekend packing for our departure. Strange as it seemed, I felt somewhat sad leaving Forest Springs. I knew I'd break away from the town someday, but I didn't expect it so soon.

Meanwhile countless questions clouded my mind. Why did Kevin Briggs finally notice me if I'd

never see him again? How could an awkward girl like me ever fit into the Fay family? What adventures lie ahead? How does it feel to fly? Would Leiko ever accept me as a sister? What will be my special power? How could I ever help others when I felt so lost myself?

"You will uncover all those answers eventually," Reva assured me.

Though I knew Mom wouldn't recall anything about me, I hoped that Grandma somehow would remember me. Regardless of what transpired in the past, I'd never forget either woman.

"We're your family now," Jessamine reminded me earlier. "You are a Fay sister forever."

"Fair Youth is now a foursome," Reva said, hugging me tightly.

Meanwhile, Leiko said nothing.

And in a quick blur, it was time to leave.

The Fay girls walked out of their home and into the dark woods. Reva, Jessamine and Leiko stood side-by-side, still as could be.

"Gentle Spirits, please protect Fair Youth as we embark on our next assignment," Reva announced.

Jessamine, Reva and Leiko suddenly lit up like blazing candles. It was the most exquisite sight I'd ever seen. Glowing light filled the woods.

Suddenly it sounded like, somewhere in the forest, someone was unwrapping paper. I looked at the Fay Girls and was startled to see them slowly sprouting magnificent wings that seemed almost too deli-
112 cate to support flight.

Jessamine's wings were golden with ornate etchings. Reva's vibrant violet wings featured intricate webbing, while Leiko's grey wings complimented her colorful hair.

"Join us," Reva commanded, as she held out her hand and I took it.

I nodded at Jessamine who carried Jake carefully. Then I glanced one final time at Forest Springs and bid it goodbye forever.

Before I realized it, I was catapulted into the dark, unknown sky toward our next mission, toward my new future.

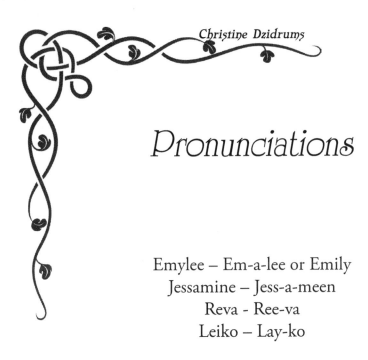

Christine Dzidrums

Pronunciations

Emylee – Em-a-lee or Emily
Jessamine – Jess-a-meen
Reva - Ree-va
Leiko – Lay-ko

About the Author

Christine Dzidrums holds a bachelor's degree in Theater Arts from California State University, Fullerton. She previously wrote the biographies: *Joannie Rochette: Canadian Ice Princess, Yuna Kim: Ice Queen, Shawn Johnson: Gymnastics' Golden Girl* and *Nastia Liukin: Ballerina of Gymnastics*. Her first novel, *Cutters Don't Cry*, won a 2010 Moonbeam Children's Book Award in the Young Adult Fiction category. She also wrote the tween book, *Fair Youth*, and the beginning reader books, *Timmy and the Baseball Birthday Party* and *Timmy Adopts a Girl Dog*. Christine also authored the picture book, *Princess Dessabelle Makes a Friend*. She recently competed her second novel, *Kaylee: The 'What If?' Game*.

www.ChristineDzidrums.com

Also From

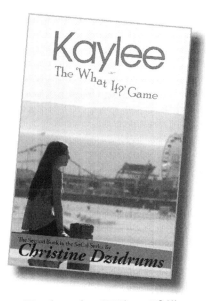

**2010 Moonbeam
Children's Book Award Winner!**

In a series of raw journal entries written to her absentee father, a teenager chronicles her penchant for self-harm, a serious struggle with depression and an inability to vocally express her feelings.

"I play the 'What If?'" game all the time. It's a cruel, wicked game."

Meet free spirit Kaylee Matthews, the most popular girl in school. But when the teenager suffers a devastating loss, her sunny personality turns dark as she struggles with debilitating panic attacks and unresolved anger. Can Kaylee repair her broken spirit, or will she forever remain a changed person?

Meet four-and-a-half-year-old Timmy Martin! He's the biggest baseball fan in the world.

Imagine Timmy's excitement when he gets invited to his cousin's birthday party. Only it's not just any old birthday party... It's a baseball birthday party!

Timmy and the Baseball Birthday Party is the first book in a series of stories featuring the world's most curious little boy!

Meet **Princess Dessabelle**, a spoiled, lonely princess with a quick temper. When she orders a kind classmate to be her friend, she learns the true meaning of friendship.

BUILD YOUR SKATESTARS™ COLLECTION TODAY!

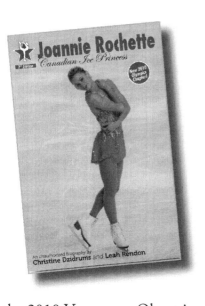

At the 2010 Vancouver Olympics, tragic circumstances thrust **Joannie Rochette** into the international spotlight when her mother died two days before the ladies short program. The world held their breath for the bereaved figure skater when she competed in her mom's memory. Joannie then captured hearts everywhere by courageously skating two moving programs to win the Olympic bronze medal. *Joannie Rochette: Canadian Ice Princess* profiles the popular figure skater's moving journey.

Meet figure skating's biggest star: **Yuna Kim**. The Korean trailblazer produced two legendary performances at the 2010 Vancouver Olympic Games to win the gold medal in convincing fashion. *Yuna Kim: Ice Queen*, the second book in the **Skate Stars** series, uncovers the compelling story of how the beloved figure skater overcame poor training conditions, various injuries and numerous other obstacles to become world and Olympic champion.

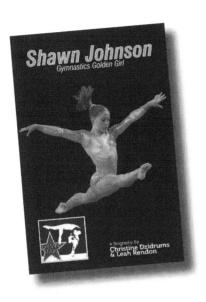
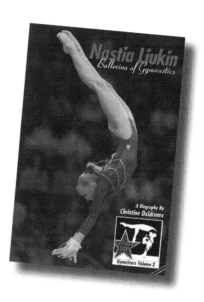

24113247R00066

Made in the USA
Lexington, KY
05 July 2013